AF420791

Ties THE SEASON

a ties world christmas novella

DANDA K.

Published December 2022

Copyright © 2022 by Danda K.

All rights reserved. No part of this book may be reproduced in any form or by any electronic or mechanical means, including information storage and retrieval systems, without written permission from the author, except for the use of brief quotations in a book review.
NOTE: This is a work of fiction. Names, characters, places, brands, media, and incidents are either the product of the author's imagination or are used fictitiously. The author acknowledges the trademarked status and trademark owners of various products referenced in this work of fiction, which have been used without permission. The publication/use of these trademarks is not authorized, associated with, or sponsored by the trademark owners.

Ties The Season: A Ties World Christmas Novella

Editor: Brandi at My Notes in the Margin

Proofreader: Tegan Reichuber

Cover Designer: Graphics by Stacy

Formatting: Brandi at My Notes in the Margin

Photo: Shutterstock

ISBN

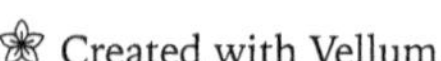 Created with Vellum

TIES THE SEASON

A TIES WORLD CHRISTMAS NOVELLA

DANDA K

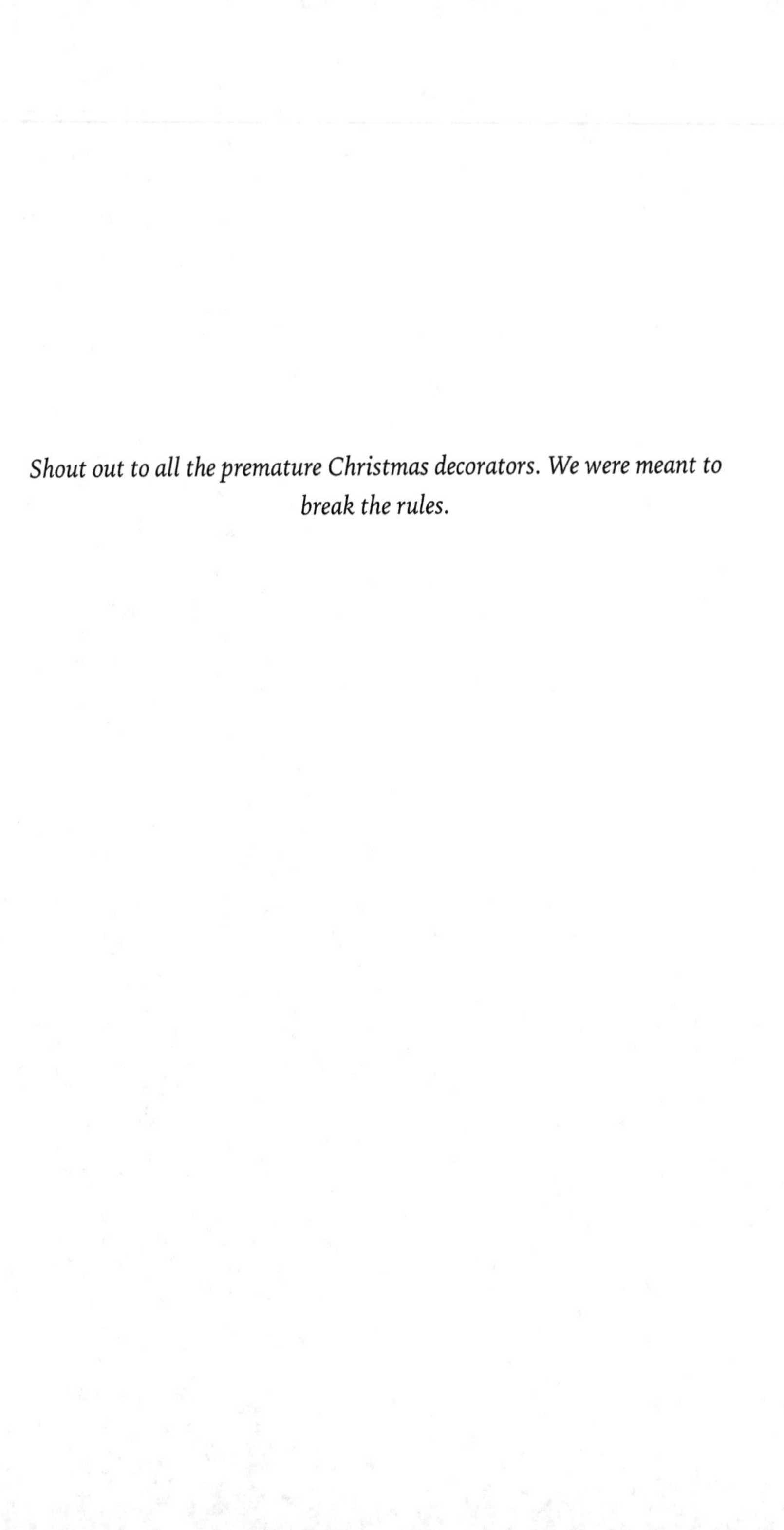

Shout out to all the premature Christmas decorators. We were meant to break the rules.

1

———

JAXON

"I'M DREAMING OF A WHITE CHRISTMAS"

"Daddy, Daddy, Daddy!" Emersyn's voice cries out from a distance, but I'm too damn tired to do anything but roll over onto my stomach.

I've spent the entire night wrapping over forty-seven presents—because as good as Cameron is at being a wife and mother—she sucks at playing elf.

The bed dips, and that's when I hear two sets of footsteps enter the room.

"Daddy, Mama. Wake up. It's Christmas." Tiny hands push at my back. "I slept all night like you said and even woke the twins up early so you don't have to...see."

One eye opens to find four big blue ones staring up at me from the side of the bed. Scarlett's dark hair is a disheveled mess as she hugs her Jets blanket, and Maverick is sucking on the same binky I could've sworn we weaned him off of over a week ago.

"Nyx..." I groan, reaching over to shake her. "Your children need you."

Cameron stirs awake. "What time is it?"

"It's already six-thirty-five," Emersyn states proudly, making me fully regret teaching her how to read a digital clock.

"Oh, angel. It's so early," Cameron mumbles as she attempts to sit up. "And we have so many people coming here later."

I follow behind and lean against the headboard, pulling both two year olds onto the bed one by one until we're all huddled under the blanket.

"But Santa came. He even brought the snow," Emersyn says with that undeniably cute lisp of hers. "And like a million presents."

It sure felt that way wrapping them.

I glance out the bedroom window to find at least eight inches of snow covering the glass, along with straggling flurries dancing with the break of sunrise in the distance.

Santa brought a fucking blizzard.

"A million?!" My mouth drops open. "Who are all these presents for?"

"Me, of course." She beams.

No. My daughter's not spoiled at all.

"Only for you, huh?" Cameron tickles Emersyn's sides, making her laugh.

"I'm pretty sure there's presents down there for your sister and brother too." I pat the twins' heads, who are still groggy from sleep. "I think my boy Maverick here already has one in his mouth." My gaze darts to Cameron, who eyerolls my accusation. "Looks like Mama caved and gave your brother back his binky."

Cameron looks down at Emersyn with a saccharine sweet smile. "Yes, and when Daddy is the one waking up with your crying brother in the middle of the night, he can have an equal opinion on the pacifier debate." She pauses, raising an eyebrow. "Plus, anything goes on Christmas, right?"

God she's sexy when she uses my words against me.

"Absolutely anything," I confirm. "Including a huge breakfast."

As if calling touché, Cameron nods before scooping Emersyn up in her arms to get off the bed. "Alright, what're we having, little miss?" Their foreheads touch. "You're the boss."

"Christmas pancakes!" Emersyn shouts, bouncing in Cameron's arms.

Christmas pancakes consist of a lot of batter, red and green food coloring, and colored sprinkles. A little tradition the Carters picked up as Emersyn got older and learned how to demand, well, *everything*.

"Christmas pancakes!" I growl in my monster dad voice, throwing my legs over the side of the bed and standing. After a quick stretch, I reach over to pick up the twins in each arm, planting a kiss on their necks before adding, "And a shit ton of coffee."

"Swear jar!" Emersyn points a judgmental finger at me. "Daddy said a bad word."

Cameron is already tossing daggers my way, but I won't let it sour the mood. Today is my favorite holiday, and now that I'm awake and coherent, I fully intend on being as extra as humanly possible to drive everyone around me completely crazy during our Christmas party tonight.

"Nuh-huh." I shake my head. "Like Mama said, anything goes on Christmas." I wink. "Even the swear words."

"Speaking of swear words," Cameron returns, "one of them decided to scratch up Grandpa's gift." She eyes something on the floor next to her, right before Magnet appears sashaying out of the room. "Maybe you should take him outside with you while you shovel the front of the house."

"I actually wasn't planning on shoveling."

"Well, you are now," she counters, still trying to appear annoyed by my language and cat. "Make a path for guests before the snow freezes up. I'll get breakfast going so we can open all those presents."

"Do those pretty lips of yours have any other demands for

me, Nyx?" I ask slyly as I circle the bed, face widening into a grin with every step closer to her.

Cameron taps her chin with an Emersyn free hand as I stop in front of them. "There is one thing, actually," she announces, those dark eyes glistening as they lock with mine. "But it doesn't involve words."

"*Now* we're talkin', baby." I lower myself to find her ear. "So, what is it?"

"Look up," Cameron whispers, and when I straighten I find her on her tiptoes, holding the mistletoe Emersyn made in school over our heads.

"It means you have to kiss us!" Emersyn giggles.

"Is that so?" I plant a huge kiss on her cheek, then do the same to the twins as they rest their heads against my shoulders. Finally, as Emersyn watches with excitement, I lean over to Cameron, our lips pressing together as I say, "Merry Christmas, Mrs. Carter."

2

MORGAN

"ALL I WANT FOR CHRISTMAS IS YOU"

There's an alarm ringing somewhere. I can't see it but I can hear it. Which means it's at least the second time it's gone off and Kim chucked her phone somewhere across the room. I watch as she rolls onto her stomach and punches the pillow to get comfortable.

"Turn that shit down." She groans, throwing the blanket over her head.

"It's seven in the morning on Christmas, savage girl. You gotta get up."

I mean, I'm up before six every morning for my workout, so Christmas makes no difference to my schedule, really. Even with all the snow that decided to make an appearance.

Kim has remained the complete opposite throughout the years, except she's even worse on holidays. It's as if she feels entitled to sleep later because the rest of the country has the day off, and there's very little that can persuade her to get out of bed.

I should know because I've already tried most of them: jumping up and down on the mattress, cold water, food, money —which she took by the way—I even sunk low enough to blast

Machine Gun Kelly over the speakers. That earned me a slap to the nuts I'm still recovering from.

"The fuck I do, you had me up all night."

Okay, that's fair. But still no.

"You weren't complaining when you were getting nice and cozy on Santa's lap."

I may or may not have dressed up as a sexy Santa in the middle of the night, and may or may not have designated her my bratty elf.

Not that Kim needs help being a brat.

She comes naturally equipped with that talent.

"Ughhhhh." She flings a pillow at me, which I dodge with no effort, then climb smoothly onto the bed until I'm towering over her sleepy naked delectable body.

"Not a fucking chance, Brookes," Kim warns, already suspecting my move and trying to awkwardly push me off from her face-down position.

I'll comply this time. Only because today's a big day.

"We got presents to open and places to be, Pereira." I slap her ass over the blanket. "And you know Cameron will hand you your ass on a Cocomelon if you make us late to another one of their holiday soirees."

"You really need to stop watching that show with their kids."

"If you must know it's highly educational, plus, it earned me the cool uncle badge."

Oh yeah, it's a real thing. Emersyn painted it herself with one of Tegan's nail polishes.

I climb off Kim and roll onto my back, staring up at the ceiling in nothing but a pair of flannel pajama pants and a growing hard-on.

"Right." Kim turns on her side to face me, curls hidden behind a silk sleep cap, a new-ish upgrade from the bandana. "The cool uncle vibes is exactly what you're achieving as you memorize songs from a toddler TV show."

It's a shame she looks so cute in that "Little House On The Prairie" hat, it makes me almost feel bad about what I'm about to say.

"And what does the wicked aunt of Williamsburg suggest they listen to?" Not that I really need to ask. She's sat the twins down in their highchairs on multiple occasions going over all the ways Pantera has changed the course of heavy metal history.

It's probably one of the reasons Jax and Cam rarely ask us to babysit. That and the colorful vocabulary words Emersyn goes home saying.

The insult results in a slap on the side of the head.

"A wicked aunt who'll make sure those kids get exposed to real music. Not that alternative emo crap Cameron and Jaxon listen to."

I'm not even going to touch this subject. Not if I want to actually get her out of this room. A thrash metal debate can easily turn into an all day lecture once she gets going.

"Whatever you say. Now uppity up, savage G." I kick my legs over the bed and stand to my full height, eyeing the digital clock, knowing in a matter of thirty-seven seconds she won't have a choice but to get her ass up.

"Fine." She huffs, rolling back onto her stomach. "Can you at least give me five more minutes?"

Sure thang chicken wang.

"Of course I can give you five more minutes," I say in my most convincing tone, bending over to pull one of my white T-shirts out of the nightstand drawer.

Just as I'm pulling my second arm through the sleeve, fate intervenes, appearing as a knock at the bedroom door.

"Kimberly." Another knock. "It's me, Daniel."

As if anyone else would be knocking on our door this early in the morning.

Kim blows out a breath, somehow managing to forget the

time stickler in the other room, who already has the entire morning mapped out for us.

"It's seven-oh-five and Austin is almost here," Daniel continues, even though neither of us have responded. "He said he'd like some pancakes, and I agree."

I chuckle watching Kim curse under her breath, knowing she can spin her way around my time schedule, but stands no chance at a dance with Daniel's.

"Since when does Texas get a say in what we eat for breakfast?" She frowns.

"Since he went out of his way to buy Daniel that iPhone."

Now we get all my brother's requests in the form of text messages and a joint calendar app. Which is the exact reason Kim and I were holding off on upgrading him from the flip phone he picked out years ago.

Guess who doesn't get these requests, though.

The asshole who got him the fancy phone.

"Who's idea was it to adopt the cowboy again?" she grumbles.

"It was Morgan," Daniel answers from behind the door. "And in case you're wondering. It's seven-oh-six."

"Alright, alright your highness. I'm getting up." She throws the blanket off her, revealing her naked body and the only present I'm looking forward to getting today.

Which is quickly covered back up with an oversized band tee.

Well, fuck you too, Led Zeppelin.

When Kim is fully dressed in sweats and a pair of socks, I sneak up behind her and wrap my arms around her waist, watching in the mirror as she carefully tames her curls.

"So, what does a savage girl like you end up asking Santa for Christmas?" I ask, burying my nose in her hair.

Turning her body to gaze up at me, Kim interlocks her

fingers behind my neck. "I'm gonna take a swing and vote for nothing, since technically she's Jewish."

I pin her with a look.

"Fine..." She huffs, bored with the question. "A pony."

"Shit. That's easy. I'm already hung like a horse."

Kim snickers as a finger skates down my chest, stopping at my torso.

I tuck a curl behind her ear. "So, tell me, how can I make the first white Christmas in decades even better?"

Even though I already know exactly how I'll be making it amazing.

She exhales a long breath, arms wrapping around my back for a hug as she says, "Honestly, rich boy, every day with you is already pretty awesome."

"Is this when I tell you to hold my non-alcoholic beverage?"

"This is when you kiss me and tell me how much you love me."

Lifting her chin with my knuckle, I place the softest kiss to her lips before I say, "I fucking love you, baby. Merry Christmas."

"Merry Christmas, rich boy." Kim bumps her nose with mine. "And I love you, too."

Another knock comes from the door, this time followed by a mouth full of food and southern accent. "Enough humpin' and bumpin' love birds, you got hungry brothers out here waitin' for some damn pancakes. And some presents."

3

———

TEGAN

"RUN RUN RUDOLPH"

The cold air sends a deep chill through me as I pull open my bedroom window, making handfuls of white powder fall onto my feet and carpet. The forced air in my building is so strong it has me frequently choosing between freezing to death or burning to death. Today I'm choosing to die by ice.

Everything outside is blanketed in so much snow I can smell the fresh, cool scent of it from my fifth floor apartment.

It hasn't snowed on Christmas in New York City in at least twenty years, a fact that would make most of the people who've been making songs and dreaming about this very moment excited about the little treat.

I am not most people, though, because unlike those nine to fivers and weekday workers, us freelancers don't have the luxury to be off on holidays. Especially not when their rent is about to get raised. Again.

I have two clients wanting makeup and hair done for their Christmas family reunion out in Dyker Heights, Brooklyn, which would be a half hour commute by bus on an average day. But today is no average day.

One, it's Christmas, the most commercialized holiday of the

year, also when the MTA prides itself on their bus schedules running half freaking assed—add on about twelve inches of snow to the mix—and I should've left the apartment two hours ago to make it to the Dornan's house on time.

I turn to my occupied bed, squeezing my fluffy robe tight around my waist as I take in the strange man snoring away.

Jim, was it? Jerry?

Eh, what does it matter when Jamal needs to get his ass up and out of my apartment within ten minutes if I want to stand a chance at making it to work only a *little* late.

As opposed to a lot of late obviously.

"Heyyo, Santa!" I bend over to pick up his red pants and toss them onto his bare back. "Time to get up, this girl's gotta work."

Yeah, so I may have picked up a bell ringing Salvation Army Santa last night. No judgy judgy now, I made sure to donate first.

"It's Christmas." The man who's name I cannot remember groans into the pillow. "Who the hell works on Christmas?"

"Santa, for starters, handsome." I toss the jacket next, not needing to bother with the hat since weirdly enough it's still on the guy's head.

He rolls onto his back and stretches, and boy am I thankful he still looks as good as he did last night when I left Henry's Pub's Christmas Eve bash. "Technically, Santa works the night before."

"Look, Josh."

"It's Jason," he mutters.

Oopsie shitsies.

"Right, of course, *Jason*." I clear my throat. "I don't have time to argue holiday semantics with you because I have to be on the other side of the borough in less than an hour."

He casts a glance out the opened window. "Yeah, hate to be the bearer of bad news, but you're not making it on time."

I roll my eyes. "I definitely won't if you don't get that sexy toned ass of yours out of my bed and on your way."

Throwing his legs over the bed, Josh, *I mean Jason dammit,* rises to his feet and gives it a good stretch before gathering his clothes.

I know I shouldn't be gawking at the guy this way since I have places to go and people's faces to glam up but seriously… when did the Salvation Army start making them look so good?

"Can I at least take a piss before the walk of shame?"

I pry my eyes off his waist as he pulls the red pants up. "Uh, yeah, sure." I offer an uncomfortable smile. "Bathroom is right across the hall."

"I remember. We had a pretty good time in there."

Must not have been that great since I can't even remember it. Granted I was pretty wasted but still, Tegan *never* forgets a really good time.

"Oh, duh." I play along, wiggling my eyebrows. "How can I forget what you were doing to me over the sink."

He blinks. "You mean the shower?"

Get your shit together, Tegan.

"Come to think of it, you're probably better off pissing outside. It melts the snow." I pull the disheveled Santa by his arm through the threshold of my bedroom into the hall.

"So, can I see you again, beautiful?"

Damn that question.

I continue dragging him along as I say, "Uhm, sure, give me a call sometime."

"But you never gave me your number."

"Right." I slap my palm to my forehead. "That's because my phone broke."

Said phone starts ringing immediately after that statement, proving how much the universe hates liars with pink hair and amazing fashion skills.

Shitsies squared.

"Uh, it's not what you think…" I attempt to save face, but by the look on my overnight guest's face he's had enough of my excuses.

"All good. A guy can take a hint, I'm outta here."

"Sorry Jacob," I say honestly, twisting the lock off the door and pulling it open. "It's not personal."

"It's *Jason*," he corrects me again, annoyed this time, and I offer him a hasty wave as he leaves.

"Merry Christmas, Jason!" I squeak, then slam the door shut.

Running back to my phone, I pick it up only a second too late.

It's my mother, of course, because only she would know exactly how to call at the worst time without even trying.

I wait for the joint voicemail I know will come from her and Dad, and when the little ding goes off on my phone, signaling a voicemail, I open the app to listen.

The usual "we miss you so much" and "Merry Christmas" and "your present will be there soon" are all included in the message, along with their report on how beautiful whichever country they're in at the moment is.

This time it's Zimbabwe.

Closing out the message, I haul ass back to my room where I throw on the first outfit I can find. Ripped jeans and an off-the-shoulder oversized sweater, along with my pink combat boots. After doing the best I can with my hair and makeup in five minutes, I'm gathering my cosmetic travel bags and rolling them both toward the front door.

Shooting my shot with an Uber, because I refuse to bother Tank on Christmas, I order a car and hope like hell they can get me to Dyker Heights faster than a bus can.

I make my way across the fifth floor hall, to the elevator, down the elevator, and to the foyer of my building in record time. Parking my ass on one of the steps in front of the exit, I wait patiently for Rob, my Uber driver to show up.

When ten minutes pass I grow impatient, deciding now would be a good time to make my morning calls to the besties.

Kimmy's first, and she picks up on the third ring as jolly as ever.

"Kill me now," she whines. "He's playing Michael Bublé."

"Merry Christmas, Kimmy!" I sing, so happy to hear her voice since I don't get to see her as much as I used to with her living in Williamsburg with her little family and all that.

"Not you too." Kim groans this time. "You're both around Jaxon way too much. I'm cutting you off."

"Aw, c'mon. It can't be that bad."

"He dressed up as Santa last night, Tegan."

Who does she think gave Morgan the idea?

"You rode on Santa's sleigh too?!" I giggle. "We're sex twinning, Kimmy!"

"Oh my God. You're worse than Morgan."

"It's only 'cause we love you."

"So you slept with a shopping mall Santa or something?"

Oh, that sounds a lot less pathetic. I'll go with that.

"Yup! Totally."

There's a beat of silence on the other end until she says, "Tegan, we've been best friends since elementary school. I know when you're lying."

She always does.

"Fine…it was a Salvation Army one."

"Tegan! Seriously?"

Another call comes through on my phone, and when I look at the screen I see it's Cameron to my rescue.

"Kimmy, gotta go, the other bestie is-a calling. Merry Christmas, I'll see you tonight!"

Kimmy blows out an exaggerated breath before offering me her version of a merry grumble as I swap the call.

"Merry Christmas Cam!" I exclaim, waving to Mrs. Neval, my neighbor, as she passes.

"Merry Christmas, T!" There're little voices screaming in the background as she adds, "I can't wait to see you tonight."

"Same here, bestie. I got so many presents I'm itching to give the kiddos."

She sighs. "As if they need more. There's a mountain of them surrounding my tree that still needs opening."

"Only the best for the Carter offspring."

Cameron chuckles. "Can't argue there." She pauses. "Oh! Don't forget the Eggnog. You know Jaxon loves how you make it."

"You got it."

A silver Jeep pulls up in front of the building, bouncing to a stop over the foot of snow.

There's my guy.

"Gotta go, Cam. My Uber is here to take me to work."

"That's right, you're working the family reunion today. Be careful getting there, the roads are shit."

She's such a mom. I love it.

"Will do. Kiss those babies for me, tell them auntie Tegan loves them so much and can't wait to spoil their adorable little butts."

"Okay, see you tonight, please don't be late!"

"That's Kimmy's area of expertise, Cam. Get it right."

There's that chuckle again. "True story. Love you."

The line goes dead after the abrupt sound of a baby crying. Most likely Maverick.

Love you too, bestie. See you later.

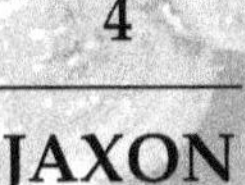

4

———

JAXON

"UNDERNEATH THE TREE"

After thirty minutes of shoveling, a bowl of spilled pancake batter, a quick clean up, another bowl of batter, a tower of colorful pancakes, and feeding a swarm of hungry children and a spoiled feline, we're finally sitting down around the tree to open presents.

"Who gets to open the first one?" Emersyn asks, even though we all know she's hoping it'll be her.

"How about you three open at the same time?" Cameron suggests, taking a sip from her coffee. "This way you, your brother, and sister are all first."

Emersyn must agree, because she's already diving into the pile of presents, scaring the hell out of a sleeping Magnet under the tree as she looks for ones with her name.

Or so I thought.

"I can't *wead*, you know," she says, holding up a box labeled "Mav The Man."

"Well, I'm sorry," Cameron gasps. "We must've confused you with the fourteen year old four year old you insist you are." She places her mug on the coffee table and slides onto all fours on the floor to search under the tree.

Of course I use this opportunity to sneak a peek at that ass in those red flannel pajamas, which has stayed quite thick and juicy after the twins were born.

"I see a round one!" Cameron sings.

In turn, I respond with, "You ain't kiddin'."

Falling back on her haunches, holding Mavericks wrapped basketball, Cameron slaps my leg.

"Here, baby." She hands the gift to our son, who's already trying to pry it open, so I scoot down next to him on the floor and prop him on my lap.

Cameron grabs a couple more presents and distributes them evenly amongst the kids, including Magnet's new Tuna toy, then pulls Scarlett to her side so she can help her.

"Alright, open them up."

Emersyn already has her princess castle open by the time we do hand over hand with the babies.

"Buh!" Maverick says, muffled by the binky.

I pull the pacifier out of his mouth. "That's right, my man. *Ball.*" I articulate the word.

After a minor meltdown of taking away his only calming source, we're back to opening the shit ton of presents taking up our living room.

The wood fire burns bright, the festive music plays low, and by the end of "I'll Be Home for Christmas" by Bing Crosby, all that's left is a single present for Cameron, which our daughter will be giving to her.

It's been a long time coming after everything that's happened to us the past few years. But now all is calm and bright and right in the world, so there's only one thing left to do to make this shit *offi-shee-al.*

"Is it time?" Emersyn whispers in my ear, and when I nod she giggles and runs over to Cameron's blue stocking, returning with a thin rectangular present wrapped in shiny red paper.

"This is for you, Mama." She hands Cameron the gift. "It's from me."

"From you, huh?" she asks from the couch, picking Emersyn up onto her lap, the both of them twinning in matching pajamas. "Then I know it must be awesome."

"It is," Emersyn confirms. "But you have to open it!"

With a kiss to Emersyn's hair, Cameron rips open the paper to find a small envelope taped to a larger manilla envelope.

"What's this?" she asks, looking between Emersyn and me.

"I wrote you a *wetter*." Emersyn's smile is wide. "Well, Daddy did. I told him what to *white*."

Yup, with only a few daddy modifications.

Cameron snickers from Emersyn's lingering baby talk. So do I. We'll both need it for when she starts reading what our daughter has to ask.

"I can't wait to see what it says." She reaches for the envelope, opens it, and pulls out the folded paper, leaving the rest of it next to her on the couch.

"Read it out loud," I instruct. "So we all can hear."

Cameron unfolds the letter and clears her throat before starting.

"HI, MAMA. IT'S ME, EMERSYN ANGEL. I'M WRITING YOU THIS LETTER TO TELL YOU ALL THE TIMES I LOVE YOU."

Cameron pauses, already getting worked up.

"I LOVE YOU WHEN YOU READ TO ME EVERY NIGHT AND TELL ME IT'S OKAY TO DRESS UP AS A FOOTBALL PLAYER EVEN THOUGH IT'S NOT GIRLY. I LOVE YOU WHEN YOU GIVE ME BATHS AND BLOW ALL THE BUBBLES IN THE AIR. I LOVE YOU WHEN YOU SING AS YOU COOK FOR US.

YOU ALWAYS LET ME BE YOUR HELPER EVEN THOUGH I MAKE A MESS."

Tears are falling steadily from Cameron's eyes, but she continues anyway.

"I LOVED YOU WHEN YOU GAVE ME MY BROTHER AND SISTER AND WHEN YOU LET ME TAKE CARE OF THEM. I LOVE YOU WHEN YOU SQUEEZE ME TIGHT AND TELL ME I'M YOUR ANGEL. I LOVE YOU WHEN YOU ASK ME TO CLEAN UP MY ROOM, EVEN IF IT MAKES ME REALLY MAD. BUT I LOVE YOU MOST BECAUSE YOU'RE MY MOMMY. I HEARD DADDY TELL UNCLE MORGAN IT'S BECAUSE YOU CHOSE TO BE. I KNOW I DIDN'T GROW IN YOUR BELLY, AND SOMETIMES IT MAKES ME SAD, BUT DADDY TOLD ME NOT ALL LOVE STORIES BEGIN THAT WAY."

Cameron takes another break, trying to hide her tears as she buries her face in her hands. Emersyn reaches up to hug her and kiss her cheek. That's all it takes for me to get choked up too.

I'm so proud of my girls, for so many different reasons, and I'm so fucking lucky I get to call them mine.

"*Pwease* continue, Mama. I want you to hear how it ends." Emersyn pleads.

Cameron nods through a sob, and plants a kiss on her nose. Taking a deep inhale, she picks up the paper again, and continues to read out loud.

"I KNOW OUR LOVE STORY IS DIFFERENT, AND OUR FAMILY IS SPECIAL BECAUSE OF IT. BUT I STILL ASKED IF THERE WAS A WAY TO MAKE YOU BECOME MY MOMMY, JUST LIKE MY BROTH—"

Cameron blows out a shaky breath, trying her hardest to keep it together.

"JUST LIKE MY BROTHER AND SISTER. HE SAID THAT YOU ARE ALREADY MY MOMMY, BUT I STILL WANT YOU TO KNOW I CHOOSE YOU TOO. I WANT YOU TO ALWAYS BE MY MOMMY, SO PLEASE OPEN UP THE FOLDER BECAUSE I HAVE TO ASK YOU A REALLY BIG QUESTION."

Emersyn reaches for the manilla envelope, and Cameron is visibly shaking as she receives it, even worse as she opens it, staring at what only Emersyn and I know is in there.

"Will you *pwease* adopt me, Mama? Be my mommy forever?" Emersyn's big blue eyes stare up in awe at Cameron, who's falling apart at the seams.

"Oh, my angel, I'm already your Mama forever." She squeezes her tightly. "But I would be so honored to make it official this way."

"I more than love you," Emersyn whispers into Cameron's chest.

"I more than love you, baby girl," she whispers back, right before Emersyn reaches for the pen attached to the envelope.

"All you have to do is sign, and then you're mine."

Cameron sobs again through a laugh, and I join in as Emersyn stares proudly at her mom, unaware of the little rhyme that broke the emotional ice.

"Daddy's lawyer friend Abe already checked off everywhere you need to sign." She hands her the pen.

"Easiest decision ever," Cameron says as she puts the ink to the paper in the designated spots, not even looking it over.

After the paper is signed, I give them another minute to hug before I pick up the babies and make our way over to them, all five of us squeezed into a group hug for what feels like forever.

And what a forever it will be.

5

———

MORGAN

"THE TWELVE DAYS OF CHRISTMAS"

"Y'know, Kim. These pancakes are top notch." Austin takes a gigantic bite from his plate. "You're getting really good at making them."

You're welcome, asshole.

"Well, she has been getting plenty of practice." I wink at her.

Kim rolls her eyes, knowing exactly what I'm suggesting. Making pancakes has sort of become our kink.

Especially when I get to lick the batter off her.

Daniel stays mostly quiet, separating his pancake pieces into three's as usual.

"What's up, baby bro?" I ask through a mouthful of bacon. "Cat got your tongue or somethin'?"

"There are no cats here," he says simply, pushing more pancakes around his plate with a fork. "Just at Jaxon's, and it only bites you."

Furry little shit.

"That's because Jaxon's cat is demonic." I wipe my lips with a napkin. "And part dog."

Kim is chuckling as she polishes off her plate. "I don't know. I like him."

"Magnet lets me pet him all the time," Austin chimes in with a shrug. "It really must be you, man."

"Maybe it is." I shoot them both a sarcastic smile. "But at least I'm not the one making friends with a ball of fleas."

"I think I will bring a friend to Christmas dinner tonight." Daniel nods. "Yes. I think that's a great idea."

The entire room falls silent as Austin, Kim, and I share a puzzled look between each other. Never in the twenty plus years I've known Daniel has he spoken of any friends other than Jaxon or Chris. Let alone invite one to dinner.

It's this very reason that Kim and I decided to keep him in the continuing education course in his private school. It caters mostly to everyday socialization and simple trades to help assist in job placement.

Daniel has been doing fantastic, and even began some volunteer work with his class at Domino Park. Some students assist in gardening, others in cleaning up and recreation.

Of course Daniel put himself in charge of his very own made up division. Wildlife and Fish preservation, which mostly consists of him educating every fisherman tossing lines into the Hudson on the local sea life. None of them mind it, though. Some even go there weekly to see him.

It's been great for Daniel, but this, I will say, was not something I expected.

Kim must agree because I have to actively force her mouth closed with my hand.

"You want to bring someone to dinner? Who?" I question, still holding Kim's jaw in place.

That is, until she smacks my hand away.

"What's his name, Danny? Have we met him at your school?" She pauses, her eyes widening as she holds up a finger. "Oh, is it that guy you were paired with on the trip to the Intrepid?"

"No. Gary isn't my friend." Daniel blinks. "He doesn't even know how many tentacles the Staghorn Coral's polyps have."

Shit.

"Do I know how many tentacles the Staghorn Coral's polyps have?" I lean over and mumble to Kim, keeping a tight smile on Daniel.

"Six, dumb ass," she whispers back. "He literally went through the differences in soft and hard corals with us last week."

Nodding, I straighten in my chair. "Okay, so who is this friend?"

"Elodie."

Elodie…as in a *lady?*

My baby brother wants to bring a girl home to the family? Fuck to the hell yeah.

The responsible adult in me is sitting firmly in the chair, watching as Daniel takes his first bite of pancakes, but the proud older bro in me is mentally ten steps ahead at my nightstand drawer reaching for some Magnum wrappers he can use.

Yes, I said Magnum, because Daniel is my blood and the Brookes men aren't only way above average in height and IQ.

Which this *Elodie* girl will soon be finding out.

Responsible Morgan returns to find Kim and Austin waiting with bated breath for Daniel to elaborate.

Which he does not, at least not until Kim coaxes it out of him with carefully curated questions.

It's not every day this guy asks to bring home something that doesn't have a specific species name attached to it.

Then again…I'm assuming she's human so…yup still a species.

"Elodie knows how many tentacles the Staghorn's Coral's polyps have. So I think she should come," Daniel responds after Kim asks why he wants to invite this girl all of a sudden.

It's not a declaration of love, but I'll take it. This shit is huge.

"I think it's a great idea baby bro."

"Doesn't she have a family to celebrate Christmas with?" Kim asks, still trying to process Daniel's unexpected request.

"Her family vacations to Italy for Christmas. She doesn't like to go so she stays at home with the housekeeper."

I know the feeling, Elodie.

"Well, I'll call Cameron to let her know but I doubt she'll mind." Kim squeezes Daniel's shoulder and he nods, going back to eating.

"So, what number wheel does a man have to be in a group of couples before being considered sad and pathetic?" Austin muses, pouring an unsafe amount of syrup on top of another pile of pancakes. "Asking for a friend."

"Not sure. But *your friend* has been pretty sad and pathetic for so many worse reasons than that," I shoot back and he flips me off.

"This is exactly why your ass got coal in your stocking, right Kim?"

"Shhhh," she whispers loud enough for the entire floor to hear. "Poor guy still thinks they're tourmaline."

"When the hell did you two become best friends?" I fold my arms and lean back in the chair, staring sharply at both the traitors. "I liked it better when Kim used to beat you in arm wrestling."

"For the love of God, man, I let her win!" Austin throws his hands up. "I was trying to get in her good graces back then."

"And the crying was, what? To really sell it?"

"I had a dang eyelash in my eye."

"And I have a four incher between my legs."

Kim is trying to hide her laugh behind a cup of orange juice. "You really convinced me, Texas. So good job."

"See? At least someone appreciates the art of good acting.

Now let's hurry this meal up because I can't wait for my little brother to see the present I got him."

WE'VE GOT TO BE AT THE CARTERS NO LATER THAN three, a firm sine qua non given to me by Jaxon because of our group's full—*appreciation*—of Kim's fashionably late tendencies.

Which means I've got less than two hours to do what I've been waiting to do for weeks now.

Kim is finishing up in the shower, and just about all is set and ready to go except for a few minor details.

Like the last candle that I'm holding.

I make my way across the living room, careful not to step on the black rose petals on the carpet or knock into the light up sign next to the fireplace and Christmas tree. My hands are shaking as I place the single candle atop the mantle next to Stella's portrait.

Glancing out on the patio, I can see both Daniel and Austin hiding poorly behind a pile of snow awaiting their cue, along with the photographer actually doing a decent job of not being seen.

My first instinct was to go big or go home, but knowing the type of woman Kim is, she'd prefer this moment to be as intimate as possible.

Mostly because she dislikes people.

Sucks for those people because they'll never know what it's like to have the most beautiful girl in the world be in love with you.

I'm lucky enough to know exactly how good it feels, and only a true idiot, which the world knows I am not, would hesitate any longer before making a girl like Kimberly Pereira officially mine.

Pulling the box out of my pants pocket, I flip it open, staring down at the pear shaped diamond pavé ring I carefully picked out for her. It took weeks for me to customize it the way I wanted, even longer to find the right black diamond.

All seven carats on this ring are perfect for Kim.

Albeit, a lot bigger than I'm sure she's expecting, but I had to add a bit of my flavor to it.

I am Morgan Brookes, after all.

The penthouse is so quiet I can hear the moment the pipes stop running water, signaling she's done with her shower. It's only moments now, because the second she walks out of that bathroom she's got a note waiting for her on the bed with directions and a path of roses leading her to where she needs to be.

With me. Forever.

I place the opened box next to Stella's picture and press the button for the music, then turn to stand tall in front of the fire. The heat emitting from it adds to the nervous sweat pooling under my suit jacket.

It takes longer than expected for the sound of the door opening, but once it does I can feel the breath I didn't know I was holding leave my lungs.

I squeeze my hands together behind my back, a smile lifting my lips immediately when I see the look of confusion on Kim's face as she takes careful steps toward me, following the trail of petals.

She's dressed in the black low cut maxi dress I laid out for her on the bed, her bare feet peeking through the bottom with every step closer. The train of the dress sweeps the roses as she moves, making her look like a gorgeous dark faerie straight out of a movie.

She took some time to tame her curls, which tells me she anticipated some kind of grand gesture, maybe even this.

We've been talking about tying the knot for a while, and I

could've sworn she was expecting a ring in one of the boxes of presents when we opened them.

As if I would be that basic.

"Morgan…" Kim calls out to me nervously, her chest rising and falling just as fast as mine when she looks around at all the candles adorning the surfaces of our home.

"Yes, baby." I hold my hand out for her to hold, letting her know it's okay.

Kim never did well with an abundance of attention, she had no choice but to get used to it, though, because I only ever had eyes for her.

"What are you…" She sighs, enclosing her hand with mine as I bring her closer.

"You know exactly what I'm doing, savage girl."

"Oh my God." Her lip trembles as she eyes the box next to her grandmother's picture.

"I'm gonna say a few words, Kim, and all I need you to do is listen, okay?"

Her gaze drifts first to our twinkling black and white Christmas tree, then the photographer sneaking inside the living room, already at work snapping pictures.

I grip her chin with my thumb and forefinger, gently turning her head. "Don't worry about him, it's just us here."

"I love you so much," she admits through a haggard breath, running a hand down my suit clad chest.

"Oh, fuck do I love you too, Kim."

Something about what I said makes her laugh and cry simultaneously…her hands shaking just as much as mine.

"I'm gonna talk now, okay?"

Kim nods her head eagerly, trying to hold back more tears.

"I don't know if I told you this, but the first thing I noticed was your hair the night we met. Your wild curls bouncing underneath those headphones. You were so lost in your little world you had no idea you just brought mine to a screeching halt." I run my thumb over her full bottom lip, drinking in the sight of her so full of nerves and wonder. "I knew it was your world I wanted to be a part of from that very moment."

Kim doesn't hold back the tear rolling down her cheek. Her only response to my words is a kiss to the finger caressing her lip.

"After that night, you became my sole purpose. To be near you, impress you, satisfy you, protect you. Even though it turned out you had a sharper right hook than most guys I know."

A sad laugh ensues, and I join in.

"You never needed me, it was something I always admired about you. You needed no one, you answered to no one. It's also something that I'm most grateful for, because it meant I was the person you chose. Of everyone else in the world you could have given yourself over to, you chose the man who happened to need you the most." I lick my lips, the words rolling off my tongue much smoother now that I've started to express them. "I'm not afraid to admit I need you. I want you. I choose you. You bring out the man in me I always wanted to be. It's a kindness I don't think I can ever fully repay, but I intend on spending the rest of my life trying." Glancing over my shoulder at the photo of Stella, I add, "There was a day at the nursing home, before things got really bad with your grandmother, that one of the nurses called you out of the room for something. I don't remember what it was. Maybe paperwork." I reach for the ring and slowly bring it between us. "Point is…while you were gone she made me make her a promise."

This intrigues Kim enough to stare long and hard at the picture before dragging her attention back to me.

"Stella told me to promise, that no matter what, if I was to ask you to marry me, I'd make sure she was there to witness it."

Kim worries her bottom lip as I continue, "She told me that even if she left this world, which, given your track record, would most likely be the case." Kim chuckles, encouraging me to do the same. "She wanted me to promise that I would do everything in my power to make sure she gets to witness the most important moment in her granddaughter's life."

Kim blows her grandmother a kiss over my shoulder, her eyes glistening even more.

"So here I am, a man that is so stupidly in love with you he has his brothers hiding outside holding confetti poppers."

Kim looks out to the patio where she finds Austin and Daniel waving at her.

"So, please marry me, Kimberly Pereira, say yes to my proposal in front of your grandmother, our family, even the universe. Make me not only the most handsome man in New York City, but the luckiest."

A small smile brightens her face. "Aren't you forgetting a single very important person you need to seek permission from?"

"You think that boy'd be standing there with working legs if he didn't?" Marcos' voice comes from the back of the house, where I told him and Loretta to stay until now, and Kim's eyes immediately widen with excitement as her father reaches our side. "I gave him a hard time at first, you know, for kicks, but eventually he convinced me."

"Dad…" Kim reaches for him and Marcos nods, taking a step back, not wanting to intrude on our moment. Loretta squeals with excitement as she awaits Kim's response.

"Answer the man, filha. Go ahead. Put him out of his misery."

Kim glances up to me with a soft loving expression, nodding her head. "I'd choose you every time, rich boy. A hundred times, hell yes. I'd really love to be your wife."

Something like a yeehaw comes from outside on the patio, courtesy of my southern brother, as I slide the ring on Kim's finger.

Without even looking at the diamond, Kim's arms are around my neck and she's kissing me. A loud pop fills the air and gold flecks rain on us while everybody cheers for our happiness.

For our success.

For our happy ending.

6

———

TEGAN

"BELIEVE"

"Holy shit, girl. You really are amazing." Gertrude, one of the sisters I've been glamming up for over two hours, gasps in the mirror.

"Bitch, I wasn't lying, her Insta does her work no justice," Elsa shoots back at her sister.

Gertrude looks herself over in the standing mirror I've been working in front of. "I love how it doesn't look like I have a ton of makeup on, but yet still every flaw is covered. And the beach waves are on point."

"Well, first of all, you're gorgeous, I only extenuated all those features with a new contour highlight technique I learned at a master class recently." Spraying some last minute texturizer in Gertrude's waves, I add, "Remember, makeup only enhances the beauty that's already there. That shit goes for every woman. We're all a bunch of gorgeous bad ass bitches."

Both girls high five me and laugh, feeling empowered by the reminder.

I always want my clients to remember that every canvas is perfect in its own way, that it's not the makeup that makes anyone beautiful. It's solely a means of expression. Liberation, even.

At least that's how I feel. My clients seem to always agree or become enlightened.

"You should stick around," Elsa suggests, ringing the falling curls of her updo around her finger. "We have so many people coming over for a Christmas brunch, and I make a slammin' cranberry spritzer."

I look down at my phone, noting the time. It's only eleven-thirty, I'm sure I could stick it out a bit if I order another Uber. I already bought all the stuff I need for the eggnog, anyway.

"Hell yeah, I'm never one to say no to a party. Especially ones that have fancy spritzers or whatever as drinks instead of beer."

Both girls laugh together again, until Gertrude spins on her chair to reach out and admire my hair.

"Ugh. I wish I was bold enough to do pink."

"Like I said, it's all about expression. If you feel like you want to be pink, be pink! Who the hell can stop you?"

Both sisters share an unreadable look between each other. "Yeah, it doesn't really work that way in our family. I'd be the talk of the year if I showed up at a party with a head of hair like that."

Her original comment about the pink suddenly feels a lot less complimentary and a lot more judgmental. Like all the uplifting words I recently offered pertain only to them, and I was here solely to deliver the message.

The mood has shifted, along with the tone of my voice.

"Well, I've learned from experience that the only person's opinion you should value is your own."

Elsa huffs. "Maybe in a perfect world, Tegan. But not in ours, trust me."

Sounds like a sad world if you ask me. A sad world I've

already agreed to take part in, though, and it would be too obvious their words affect me if I decline now.

"Alright, enough with the negativities," Gertrude cuts in. "It's Christmas. Let's go get some champagne. God knows we'll need it…the family is already arriving."

Somewhere between awkward introductions to random old people, French hors d'oeuvres, which were so fan-freaking-tastic I had to snatch extra from the servers, and about three overly sweetened spritzers, I've not only lost my judgy clients and any interest in carbonated wine but track of time and the server who was feeding me the goods.

I'm usually great at bringing life to a party, but if Gertrude and Elsa were right about anything, it's that their family are a bunch of boujee duds. Maybe that's why they're in hiding.

This entire colonial home has been transformed into a winter wonderland, everyone dazzled in dresses and suits which seem more fitting for some type of gala or ball.

I make my way around aimlessly as I wait for an Uber, relieved I received payment before joining this wack ass pompous party.

I snag another *Coquilles St-Jacques* off a server's tray as she passes, but as I bring the shell to my lips I feel something hard hit me from behind, making me drop the fancy scallop on the floor when I stumble forward.

Well, fuck a duck. I've been waiting for that one to come around again, damn it.

"I'm so sorry," a smooth velvety voice says. I feel a strong hand squeezing my waist, holding me in place. "I couldn't catch my footing until it was too late."

When I turn to face the man attached to the hand, I find a drop dead gorgeous one staring down at me.

One I can already tell looks irresistible naked.

"Eh, no worries." I shrug. "There's only so many *Coqs* a girl can handle at a single party."

"*Coqs?*" gorgeous dude questions with a raised brow.

I offer him my best flirtatious grin, which he returns with one so wide it brightens his baby blue eyes. Between the shaggy short curls, dark button down, and sovereign smile, everything about this stranger screams Ryan Phillipe in *Cruel Intentions*.

Except there's no sign of a womanizer in front of me—I'd know because I've been screwed over by enough of them—instead there's an underlying sweetness about this guy I can't quite figure out.

I pop a hand on my hip, pretending like the gutter isn't my brain's best friend. "I was talking about the scallops, mister."

The both of us share a united laugh at our expenses, and when a server passes the stranger plucks two champagnes off the tray, handing me one first before taking a sip of his own.

"What's your name, handsome?" My eyes dip to the lightest dusting of chest hair peeking out of his unbuttoned shirt.

"I'm August Griffin." He holds out a hand. "And who did I have the pleasure of bumping into?"

I interlock my hand with his as I say, "That would be Tegan."

"Tegan, huh?" He releases me and smoothly slides the hand I was just holding into his slacks pocket, his delighted gaze skirting all the way down to my Docs. "Tell me, Tegan, where in the world did you come from this Christmas?"

"If I told you from one of the guest rooms would you believe me?"

"With a beautiful face like yours? Hardly."

I click my tongue. "Well, it's true. I was hired to do Gertrude and Elsa's hair and makeup for the party."

"So you're the reason my cousins are that much less revolting today?"

"Harsh." I wince, secretly bathing in the insult.

"But true," he argues, tipping his glass my way. "You met them, I'm sure you know it."

"I plead the fifth." I zip my lips closed and take a long sip of champagne.

"So you're a hair and makeup artist?" He steps closer, holding his flute between us.

"I am."

"A very talented one I see."

"Why thank you." I clink my glass with his. "It's been a long road, but I love what I do. Even if the income isn't as steady as I'd like it to be."

"Well, I've been working with Big Apple Elite Talent Agency for over ten years now as a junior agent."

"Rub it in, why don't ya?" I roll my eyes in jest.

August shakes his head. "I'm not gloating. Haven't you ever heard of B.A.E?"

"Does the look on my face imply that I have?" I point to my very uninformed wrinkled nose.

"Big Apple Elite works strictly with Broadway to find them lead actors for roles in all their shows."

I stare blankly at him, unaware of where this story is going.

"You know…*Wicked…The Lion King…Cats?*"

"I know what Broadway is, silly." I playfully shove his arm. "I just have no idea what this has to do with my finicky little job."

August inhales a deep collected breath. "Well, the stage manager Tom is a close friend of mine. They're always looking for fresh new artists to work with the smaller actors and dancers. I bet I can get you an interview." He shrugs. "If you're interested in a steady gig that is."

An interview to work on a Broadway stage? Holy shit, that's the best Christmas gift a girl like me could dream of. I could meet literal stars, make friends with celebrities, hell, maybe one day actually do their makeup if I'm lucky.

This is a no brainer.

"Are you serious? You can get me an interview?" I try my hardest not to hug the life out of this man.

"It's the least I could do for so rudely *Coq* blocking you." A playful smirk follows the awful joke.

I laugh anyway, because, *fucking Broadway baby!*

The snickers come out through a bundle of nerves and excitement, both equally powerful enough to have me wrap my arms around this gorgeous, generous, sexy man.

Who's not making me want to hop in his bed any less.

"I would so so appreciate you making that call, August. Like really, really appreciate it." I squeal, still hugging the guy but he doesn't seem to mind.

"Who said anything about making a call?"

I take a step out of the embrace, feeling like maybe this was a cruel joke of some sort.

"So you're not gonna call your friend?"

"Nope. There's no need." He takes another sip of his champagne. "Because he should be here in about ten minutes."

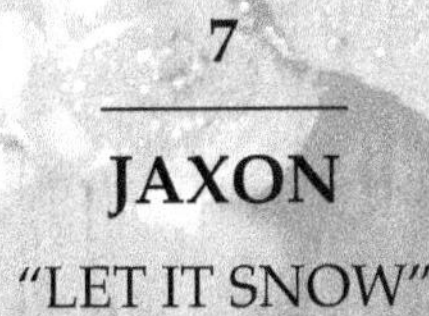

7

———

JAXON

"LET IT SNOW"

I'm feeding Scarlett her last bite of spaghetti for lunch when Cameron hangs up on a twenty minute phone call with Kim, grinning like a Cheshire cat.

"Looks like we'll be needing an extra plate at the table tonight." She places the phone down on the counter, going back to taking out the fancy Chinaware we use for holidays.

"For who? The entire family already comes every year." Scarlett starts fussing in her booster chair, so I go ahead and remove the table top and wash off her face and hands with a paper towel.

Cameron's leaning with her back against the counter when she says, "Apparently Daniel is bringing a friend with him this year."

Now *that* I was not expecting.

"That's fantastic. Damn." I huff out a laugh. "I would've figured Texas found himself a cowgirl."

"Gonna be pretty hard to find one of those in New York City," Cameron quips. "Plus, it's good for Tegan to have one of us still ridin' solo. I'd never want her to feel like she's a fifth wheel of some sort."

Pretty sure I'd prefer her alone than with the halfwits and undeserving assholes she attempts to bring around.

I say attempt because Morgan and I usually end up threatening their existence within the first hour of their "Yo, sup bro?"

"Tegan would never feel that way. She knows how much we love her."

Cameron shrugs, going back to setting up the dining room. "I know, Jaxon, but there's gonna come a day where you have to actually *be nice* to someone she brings around. Tegan deserves happiness."

"Nyx, you think I don't know that?" I argue, lifting Scarlett and placing her on the floor, watching as she runs off to find her siblings before I add, "It's *why* I want to sieve out the bullshit for her. She's too good for these tools in Coney Island."

"You may be right, but she's an adult. More than capable of making her own decisions."

Yeah, and I have nothing against Tegan's decisions as long as they aren't shit ones.

"She's also my best fucking friend, Cameron. My unbiological little sister. It's my job to look out for her."

Am I a little too protective of Tegan? Obviously, she's barely five feet or a hundred pounds soaking wet.

She's also my family. And I'll eviscerate anyone who tries to hurt my family. Unfortunately, Tegan finds herself in predicaments with guys who have the ability to do just that.

Hurt her.

I can't let that happen.

I also can't protect the tiny person from the world for the rest of my life, no matter how much I wish I could.

"Let's just be grateful it's Daniel bringing a date to Christmas dinner tonight, eh?" I wink at her and she offers a thumbs up, knowing there's no changing my mind when it comes to our miniature best friend.

"Sounds like a plan, now come set this table while I baste the ham. Thanks to your caveman tendencies, I'm five minutes too late."

For the next two hours I clean up the house, Cameron finishes up the cooking, and Grandpa Sayeed arrives with Sam holding two handfuls of presents for the kids, which he wasted no time letting them open.

We already went over the big news about Cameron adopting Emersyn, which of course he knew would be happening, and we're just settling down at the table to relax before company arrives.

"The food smells delicious Beti," Sayeed compliments Cameron as she sits exhausted next to me.

"Thank you, I've been at it since early this morning. I'm ready for bed." She laughs. "Guess that won't be an option for a while, huh?"

"How about a glass of wine to relax?" I lean over the table and reach for the Pinot, her usual go-to while she prepares any holiday feast. But surprisingly, it's still sealed.

Cameron shakes her head. "No thanks, I'm good babe. It'll make me even more tired."

Thinking nothing of it, I sit back down and take a sip from my beer.

"This is for you two," Sayeed announces, handing Cameron an envelope. "Use it however you want. Merry Christmas."

Cameron hugs the envelope to her chest, already knowing what's inside will likely be enough to buy her the new coffee maker she's been wanting. "Thank you so much, Dad." She stands, making her way around the table to hug Sayeed. "You're the best."

"Of course Beti, spend it well." Sayeed hugs her back.

"Dada!" Emersyn shouts from the living room, surrounded by her brother and sister. "Come play with my new Barbie Dreamhouse with me!"

Sayeed blows out a breath, pressing his palms on the table before standing. "If someone told me ten years ago there would come a time I'd be playing with Barbie dolls I would tell them they went mad."

"Yet here you are, Pops." I cross my arms, leaning back in the chair. "About to live the plastic dream."

"Leave him alone." Cameron swats my arm. "It's not in a grandpa's nature to say no."

"And boy does my little Poti know it." Sayeed takes off, passing Sam on the couch who's busy playing on his cell phone.

"Yo, earth to Mister 'I'm Too Cool To Play With Toys', get over here and give me a hug."

Rolling his eyes, Sam stands, almost a whole foot taller than he was when I first met Cameron, and grumbles the entire way over to me.

"You're gonna be taller than Dad soon." I pull him onto my lap and scruff his messy black hair. "What's so important on your phone that you can't hang with us."

"Playing Roblox."

"*Playing Roblox*," I echo, teasing him. "Thought maybe you got a girlfriend on that phone I don't know about."

Sam grins mischievously, leaning closer. "I've got a few actually."

"Ha, my man!" I high five him and Cameron rolls her eyes, assuming what was said.

There's rubbing at my feet, and when I look down I find Magnet looking at me, matching yours truly in his ugly Christmas sweater, except my bells are hanging off my boots not a collar.

"Right now? Really?" I ask him, and he continues to stare at me. Little shit loves the snow and has been trying to get his ass out there all day.

I look over at Cameron and she nods, confirming she doesn't

need anything else from me. "I'm gonna go get dressed while Dad occupies the kids, anyway."

I wink at her, turning back to Magnet. "Alright you little furball, let's go. But only for a few minutes."

"You taking him out? Can I come?" Sam asks, finally looking enthusiastic about something other than the little screen he's been staring at.

"Fine. But the phone stays inside."

"Deal." He hops up, already running for the door. Magnet follows of course, because like I said earlier, anything goes on Christmas.

8

MORGAN
"SANTA BABY"

We decided to keep our announcement a secret until we arrive at Jaxon's, hoping our surprise engagement will make up for me forgetting to buy my Secret Santa gift.

Again.

I mean, Jaxon already has me as a best friend, so what other present could the fucker really need?

After finishing up our engagement photos and getting ready for the party, the seven of us ended up squeezing into my Escalade, since finding a spot in Brooklyn after a blizzard for one car is impossible enough.

With Kim at my side—Loretta, Daniel, and Daniel's new friend Elodie behind us—that left Marcos, my charming future father-in-law, along with my little southern pumpkin pain in the ass to sit bitch all the way in the back.

Oh, the glorious little victories.

It was—interesting to say the least—when we picked up our foreign guest. All five foot two of freckles and ginger hair dressed in green plaid overalls and a white turtleneck reaching just under her chin.

A coat nowhere in sight.

Which would've striked me as odd, until I remembered she was my brother's friend.

Odd is his modus operandi.

But Elodie...she wasn't what I was expecting yet somehow absolutely obvious at the same time.

The Little Mermaid is the only Disney movie Daniel ever enjoyed watching, and I know damn well it had a lot to do with the fish but A LOT more to do with the pretty mermaid wearing shells for tits.

It's also how I know his excuse for inviting Elodie tonight has nothing to do with polyps, and everything to do with the fact my brother is experiencing his second crush.

Ariel being the first.

There's nothing like a woman's instincts, though.

Back at the house Kim insisted Daniel give his lady friend a gift for Christmas, and since all of the stores are closed today for shopping, she offered up one of the graphic tees I bought her along with Daniel's newest 3D puzzle we got him for Christmas.

He protested, which only made Kim add on a bouquet of flowers that were sitting in a vase to shut him up.

Which it did, because she was adamant about it being the chivalrous thing to do and threatened to use one of his model sharks, instead.

Kim has the perfect balance of no nonsense and leniency when it comes to my brother, and for reasons I can't fathom, her methods always seem to work.

Watching him get out of the truck and hand the sweet redhead flowers like they were opponents in a game of Hot Potato was like watching the autistic version of an awkward hug.

Fucking adorable.

Until she got in the car and it went dead silent, making even Texas uncomfortable.

That is until now when Kim becomes the only one daring

enough to break the ice. Even Loretta has been shocked to silence.

She turns around in her seat to face the new girl. "So, Elodie, tell us about yourself."

"I don't like zippers," Elodie responds swiftly. "Or Machine Gun Kelly."

Oh, she'll fit right in.

"Alright." Kim purses her lips. "Well, I'm with you on the shitty rapper sister, his music sucks."

Elodie looks out the window, saying, "Daniel taught me about Pantera, I like them very much."

That is all Kim needed to hear to make her head inflate three times the size of my truck.

"He did, huh?" She shoves his knee proudly. "Smart man." She looks back at Elodie, even though the girl doesn't make eye contact. "So how did you two meet? School?"

"Yes. I started last year."

Last year, huh, which is also when Daniel started asking for a full keyboard phone. To text.

Kim seems to also be putting the pieces together as her eyes dart my way with a knowing smile.

"Well, we can't wait to learn more about you." Kim clears her throat, trying to get the rest of the car's attention, including Daniel's. "Right guys?"

As if being startled, everybody, except my brother, responds with different versions of "oh yeah" and "absolutely" simultaneously. Loretta finishes it off with a "beyond thrilled my dear".

Daniel shrugs. "I already know enough about her."

Christ, Danny.

If I could facepalm the steering wheel right now, I would.

There are low snickers in the back as Kim responds, "Trust me, Danny, I've been around your brother a long time and he still surprises me."

"I understand," he agrees. "Seeing him in a Santa costume

would surprise me too." Daniel blinks. "Especially what I heard him doing to you in it."

I practically swerve into oncoming traffic with that statement, and Kim looks like she wants to haul herself out the window as she turns her body around.

A full belly laugh erupts out of Austin from the third row, and I can feel the heat of a thousand suns piercing the back of my head.

I check the rear view mirror cautiously, only to find Marcos' murderous eyes, well, *murdering me*.

It's too late for him to take back his blessing, right?

Daniel and his friend don't seem phased by his comment one bit, and Loretta looks scared for my life as she watches Marcos watching me.

"Daniel!" Kim exclaims. "Seriously?"

"I can't help what I hear going to the bathroom at night."

That's it…he's getting an en-suite bathroom and we're getting sound proof walls. I need to fuck without judgment.

Marcos is mumbling something in Portuguese, most likely a threat, so I decide to turn on the Christmas music station.

Which is playing "Santa Baby" by Eartha Kitt.

Great.

Real funny, universe. Real fucking funny.

More Portuguese curse words ensue, and now even Kim is laughing at my expense.

I chuckle nervously, shutting off the radio with a quick push of my finger, and the rest of the drive turns to a bumpy crawl the entire way to Jaxon's.

9

TEGAN

"JINGLE BELLS"

I can barely contain my excitement as I walk through the front door of the Carters' house. I try to, though, of course because it's Christmas, a day to celebrate the winter solstice, birth of a god, not a makeup *goddess*.

Although, you won't find this goddess declining a birthday greeting or two.

I certainly did not deny the one my Uber driver offered on our way over here after I told him what happened.

First things first at the Carters', though. My babies will get their lovies from auntie Tegan before she goes spilling any kind of life changing news to their parents.

"Where's my little ducklings?!" I holler across the house as I whoosh the door closed on the blistering cold.

I don't even get the chance to stomp the snow off my boots before all three of them are barrelling toward me.

Maverick even dropped the binky from his mouth in honor of my arrival.

"Auntie Tegan!" Emersyn beams as she runs with her arms wide in a little red dress. The twins are in red too, a sweater for Maverick and a matching dress for Scarlett.

I place all the gifts, including the pitcher of eggnog, on the floor next to me before falling to my knees, scooping all three of them up in a big hug.

"Oh, I missed you little quackers. Merry Christmas." I kiss each of their heads and add, "Did Santa bring you all the best presents?"

"He got me my Barbie Dreamhouse!" Emersyn exclaims as she takes a step back. "And Scarlett a kitchen and Maverick a ball pit!"

"Wow!" I feign shock by cupping my hands against my cheeks. "Sounds like you guys rocked the heck out of that nice list."

"I always behave." Emersyn bats her eyelashes and sways, interlocking her fingers.

"Always has become quite the pliable word," Cameron muses, making my head dart up to find her and Jaxon striding over to greet me.

"Well, dayum mama!" I stand, shaking my wrist in a *Wowza!* gesture. "You look freaking hot!" Wiggling my eyebrows I say, "I'd ask what's the occasion but we both know how much you love to dress all sexy for me."

Cameron looks down at her long sleeved velvet dress, then back up at me, chuckling. "Merry Christmas, you crazy girl."

Stepping around the three children attacking the presents I bought them, I reach up and hug my best friend before offering her my signature peck on the lips. "Merry Christmas, gorgeous." I tilt my head, noticing how perfect her skin looks. "You using a new foundation or somethin'?"

Cameron presses a hand to her cheek. "Uh, yeah, how'd you know?"

"Seriously?" I raise an eyebrow. "It's literally my job to know these things."

Cameron smiles as Jaxon crosses his arms over a hideous

Christmas sweater, every year proving how much of a high key dork he is.

"Yeah, if you're done flattering my wife, I'd like some compliments too."

I eye him up and down. "I'm loving what you've done with your boots."

"It was the bells hanging off these or Jets slippers." He points to the green and white moccasin looking concoctions next to the couch.

"Those are…quite something." I try my best not to contort my features in disgust.

He grins. "They were a present from the kids. Now get over here you little minx."

Practically leaping into his arms, I squeeze Jaxon as tight as I can before rendering him the same smooch I did his wife.

"Merry Christmas to my favorite person in the whole wide world." I snicker, looking down between us. "God, your sweater is so ugly I can't take it."

Color block patterns of red and green plus the cat in the Santa hat?

Yup, I'd expect nothing less of Jaxon Carter, first of his name, father of felines, breaker of all things toxic masculinity.

"Duh. That's the point." He squeezes me back, not thinking much of the diss before setting me down. "You get here okay?"

"Oh, yeah, I gave my driver an earful of my crazy day."

"Well, I hope it was a *good* kind of crazy." Jaxon gestures with his hand for me to come in, then picks up the pitcher off the floor and hands it to Cameron so he can pry the presents out of his kids hands.

"It was a great one, actually! But I'm gonna wait for Kimmy to get here so I can tell you guys about it all at once."

Around a half hour passes as the bunch of us start to settle into our little Christmas party.

During this time, I help Cameron with last minute preparations and am greeted by Sayeed and Sam, who always get me a small gift, and Sam can never wait to give it to me. This year it's a really pretty golden brooch I didn't hesitate to pin on my sweater dress.

I absolutely love it.

"Thank you guys again for this." I run a finger over the gems. "It's stunning."

"Sam here picked it out." Sayeed nods his head toward his son whose face is reddening by the second.

I wink at Sam, which only makes his face even brighter.

"Ah, young love," Jaxon whispers next to me on the couch, and both Cameron and I slap him.

"Leave him alone," I scold him quietly, feeling sorry for the kid.

I remember what it's like to have those hormones creeping in with adolescence.

Hell, mine never left.

The doorbell rings, saving Sam any more embarrassment, and Cameron is already up and moving to the door to greet whoever it is on the other side. Jaxon is right behind her, of course.

Always the gentleman.

I look down at my phone, noting the time, and would be absolutely floored if our other bestie actually made it here through a blizzard without being late.

I hear Morgan's cackle over Jaxon's sweater first, and when I look over my shoulder I find them bro hugging, the rest of their family trailing in around them shaking off the snow.

I jump out of my seat, eager to get my hands on Kimmy so I can squeeze the heck out of the bitch. It's been six weeks since I've seen my person. We've barely gone two days apart since we met.

Kimmy's smile is prominent as I throw myself at her and kiss her hello.

"Oh, I missed you so much you cranky thot." I wrap my arms around her tighter, wanting more of my long lost bestie living her best happy life.

"I missed you too, my little pink capuchin."

"Best Christmas present ever." I squeal until Morgan pulls me off his girl like the caveman he is.

"Sup pinky?" He fist bumps me. "I'm surprised you're not exhausted from making all those toys."

Oh, Morgan and his corny jokes. His good looks must be exhausted from carrying all the weight of his ego.

He's lucky I love him, but not enough to resist throwing in a good dig when necessary.

"What a shame," I pout, batting puppy dog eyelashes at him. "All these years trying and you still haven't made it on Santa's funny list."

"Ohhh, burn." Jaxon winces and laughs. "But facts, brother. Your jokes are almost as lame as your Christmas presents."

"Uh, yeah, about that..." Morgan cringes, and I assume it's because he forgot to get his Secret Santa gift yet again.

Cameron closes the door behind everyone, retrieving all the coats as her guests take them off, and the entire crew slowly migrates toward the living room, where glasses of champagne and sparkling grape juices are waiting for the alcohol free peeps.

We offer sweet greetings, glad tidings, and happy cock ridings—*I'm almost 100% positive that's how one of those Christmas songs go*—and before we know it the excitement dies down and we begin to assess the elephant in the room.

A.K.A. the adorable girl standing next to Daniel mother-fuckin' Brookes.

My news can wait for this.

Much like her date, Elodie doesn't have a lot to say, other than to Daniel quietly as they talk amongst themselves next to the fireplace. Far away from all of us.

Oh, to be a phallus on the wall of that conversation.

I'm 100% positive that's not how *that* saying goes.

Either way, it gives us a chance to discuss the details of the adorable little *courtship* unfolding before our eyes.

"My man, don't ask me. I was just as shocked when he told us about her this morning," Morgan responds to Jaxon after he asks what the rest of us are eagerly thinking.

"It's a wonderful thing," Loretta chimes in. "Daniel would make an excellent partner, both platonic and romantic."

"I have to agree, Loretta, I've seen a lot of growth in the boy the past year." Marcos takes a bite out of some beef salami from the charcuterie board Cameron had me slice up cheese for. "A woman will always change a man." He scoops up another handful of meat off the coffee table, not bothering with the spoon or plates Cameron put out for serving. "But the right one will only change him for the better."

"It's their first freaking date and this guy is already reciting poetry on their behalf." Kim laughs at her dad, making the rest of us laugh too. "How about we just let them be and see what happens?"

Marcos concedes, going about his business with the finger foods, which allows enough beats of silence for someone to jump in with a convo starter.

Kimmy and I happen to leap at the opportunity at the same time, with the same energy, and almost the same statement of "I've got news".

Except hers includes a "we".

I turn to face her, Maverick on my lap. "You've got news too?!"

She crinkles her brows. "Yeah, what's your news?"

"Nuh-uh," I insist with a shake of my head, and so does Kim.

"You two are stubborn enough to be here all night doing this," Cameron bops Scarlett on her lap. "So one of you spill, already."

"I'm curious to know too," Sayeed says on his way back from

the kitchen with a giggling Emersyn in his arms. "Even though I wasn't really involved in the conversation."

I wave him off like he's crazy. "Are you kiddin'? Most of us like you more than Texas over here."

"Truck off," he mutters, being careful to use the only kind of safe words Jaxon and Cameron will ever bother to come up with.

"You know, I've always wondered if cowboys say 'yeehaw' for more than just being on top of *horses*…" I tap my cheek, which is spreading into a devilish grin.

"Real appropriate for Christmas," Texas shoots back. "With children around for Christ's sake."

"You know me, keepin' it classy. And, I'd hardly call you a child, Austin, more like a pubescent."

Cameron and Kim are biting back a laugh, I can't say the same for the guys. Except for Sayeed, he looks as though he just walked in on his parents going to pound town.

You'd think by now the groups designated Dad would get used to my…*keen* sense of humor.

"On that note," he says with a level of comfort that one would feel standing naked on a stage. "I'll go check on Samir and make sure he's not eating all of the cranberry pie Cameron baked."

Loretta holds up a finger, and I can taste her need for an escape on my tongue. "I better help you, uh, you know, find the pie."

"Oh, he can use a little of that American one, too." I wink at Loretta, and she strolls off with rosier cheeks than Sam had earlier.

It's safe to say everyone has accepted I'm the inappropriate friend they can't censor or get enough of.

They love me, my people.

And I love them back, so much I feel zero remorse for speaking what everyone is thinking.

Sexually that is.

"There is something fundamentally wrong with you." Jaxon shakes his head.

My head swivels his way, aghast. "You're gonna tell me it's not obvious those two secretly want to *jingle* each other's bells?"

Both Jaxon and Morgan make a gagging face before Morgan says, "Yeah, that's exactly what he's telling you."

I let out a deep rueful sigh. "I can just see it now, the love story of the century. Our modern day Aladdin finding his Cinderella." I point a judgmental finger at each of them. "Mark my words, before you donkey head's know it, those dangling bells between Sayeed's legs will be turning into wedding ones."

Kim lets out a groan as Cameron pinches the bridge of her nose.

"You literally think everyone is in love with everyone," Kim argues.

Yet no one seems to ever be in love with me.

I don't allow the thought to fester before shooing it away with my usual bright smile.

"What can I say?" I shrug. "I love love and how it's made."

Both physically and emotionally.

"And we," she gestures between her and Morgan, "would love it if you would tell us what the hell your big news is before the fat man in red comes around again."

"Okay, okay, fine. Geez. Tough crowd." I scoff. "I'd probably have a better shot with Daniel and his mermaid princess over there."

"See! I told you. She looks just like her." Morgan slaps Kim's arm, where she in turn punches his back.

Shaking my shoulders, I clear my throat. "Okay guys, so, you know how I had to work the Dornan sisters this morning?"

Everyone nods, well, except Texas and Marcos who seem to be partaking in a sausage eating contest.

Oh, now that is quite the idea for an Onlyfans page.

I put a pin in the visual of a cowboy and biker bumpin' uglies for subscribers, and get back to the announcement at hand.

"So I met a guy there..."

"I hate this story already..." Jaxon grumbles.

I slap his arm this time. "Not *that* kind of guy."

"He ugly or something?" Kim questions, a bit skeptical. "An ugly eunuch?"

"Oh no." I shake my head. "I'd fudge him fifty different ways till Sunday. He's totally hot. Definitely got a junior, too, I made sure to peep the bulge."

Kimmy and Cameron both nod in acceptance. As if now the entire story makes sense even though I haven't finished it yet.

The guys couldn't look any more disinterested in hearing another word about cockless men, though.

Real dicky downers if you ask me.

"Anyway..." I start, broadening my shoulders. "His name is August, he's some big wig at a talent agency that works closely with..." The excitement kicks in again and I squeal. "Guess!"

"Pornhub?" Morgan grunts.

"Oh! No," I say, pausing. "But that'd be freaking awesome if he did. I always wanted to audition for kicks." I sigh. "And dicks."

Jaxon rolls his eyes. "Continue please."

I thought he'd never ask.

"His company finds actors and actresses for Broadway shows! Eeep!"

The group finally looks intrigued, even Texas and Marcos are scooting closer to hear the point.

"Holy shit that is pretty cool," Cameron states, wide eyed. "So what's the big news?"

"Well, it all started when August knocked over my Coq."

Marcos nearly spits out a piece of cheese.

"Not that kind of cock, daddy biker man. Get your head out

the gutter!" Side eyeing him with a grin, I add, "I meant my fancy scallop."

"First off," Kim interjects, "You are not allowed to use the term Daddy in any sentence pertaining to my father. I know the books you read." She looks between me and Marcos, who seems as though he's finally reconsidered stuffing his face with sausage. "Second off, just get to the part where we know what the hell you're getting at. I have images in my head that I need to burn now thanks to you."

I guess that's fair, she knows I ride that daddy kink train.

Alright, fine, I'm the conductor, whatever.

"Okay, okay. So. August knocked over my..." I eye Marcos carefully. "Scallop. After he apologized we ended up talking. Turns out one of his close friends is the stage manager on Broadway. He offered to get me an interview with him for a makeup artist position."

Each and every one of my friends are out of their seats with shock and excitement. A mix of "that's amazing", "holy shirts", and even the actual curse word coming out of Jaxon's mouth.

"That is freaking awesome, T!" Cameron hugs me. "I know you'll nail that interview."

"Oh, you bet your fine *ash* I will! Because August's offer wasn't the best part."

"Well, what the hell is?" Kim asks, practically shaking from anticipation.

"The guy was at the party. I met him, and we hit it off! I have to go for a formal interview but from how he made it sound after seeing the work I did on my clients, it's really just a formality!"

"Oh my God!" The girls are jumping up and down, Scarlett looking more like a rag doll in Cameron's arms.

Kimmy sits down next to me again to squeeze me into a sideways hug. "I'm so fucking proud of you bestie." She whispers, adding, "You deserve this more than anyone."

"Thanks Kimmy." I lean my head against her shoulder and smile down at my little man Maverick. "It's the second greatest gift the universe has ever given me."

We both know what the first one was.

My only hope is that the universe isn't cruel enough to take this one away from me too.

10

JAXON

"HAVE YOURSELF A MERRY LITTLE CHRISTMAS"

After the emotion dies down from Tegan's news, Sayeed, Sam, and Loretta start trickling in from the kitchen with the rest of us settling around the fire before dinner.

"Okay, Kimmy, your turn," Tegan suggests with a squeeze to her friend's knee. "What's the big news?"

I'm trying to wrap my head around what could be so important that it has Kim actually wanting to draw attention to herself.

Our USA Today and New York Times Best Selling author usually has more to say behind paper and pen.

Kim shares a questionable glance with Morgan before saying, "Oh, it's actually nothing. It can wait."

"The *truck* it can!" Tegan insists. "I told you my good news, now we want to hear yours!"

A small smile spreads Kim's lips. Morgan's too as they agree. "Well, it's not really something to be told…more like shown." Kim reaches inside her pocket, pulling something out of it.

"Oh my God!" Both Cameron and Tegan scream in unison, as if putting two and two together.

I can't say the same for me.

Until I see a huge black diamond ring appear in Kim's hand, and Morgan does the honor of sliding it on her finger.

No motherfuckingway.

Morgan proposed.

I'm absolutely flabbergasted, not because I didn't think he had it in him, but because my best friend is so excessive I totally expected this moment to come with a parade of elephants and gold writing in the sky.

Christmas is so…chill for such an audacious guy like Morgan.

Then again, who needs the glory of materialistic things when you can have the simplicity of meaningful things?

The love of a woman.

Especially a strong woman like Kim.

"I can't *trucking* believe it! Ahhhh!" Tegan yelps as she jumps into Kimmy's arms like a giddy school girl. "My person is marrying her person."

Cameron joins in on the hug, the three of them huddling together in a fit of excitement as they examine Kim's gigantic ring, and I make my way over to my best friend.

"Congratulations brother." I clap him on the back. "I'm happy for you both, truly."

Sayeed offers his congratulations to the both of them, Sam and new girl Elodie too, until finally Cameron says, "You need to tell us everything! How did he propose?"

Everyone takes the cue to sit back down, and Kim doesn't start explaining until Cameron and I get the kids settled with some toys so we can focus.

"It was really intimate, which I'm grateful for, but so magical," she starts, squeezing Morgan's hand. "I was in the shower as he prepared everything in the living room. From the candles taking up every surface, to the roses, even the music was on low playing "I Guess I'm In Love" by Clinton Kane."

"Oh my God," both girls practically moan.

"You set up an entire house that fast?" I ask, astonished. Showers are what? Maybe ten minutes?

"I had help," Morgan replies adoringly, staring down at Kim. He looks my way from the corner of his eye. "And have you witnessed one of this girl's showers? They're longer than my…" He looks over at the kids. "You know."

"Haha, it's true," Cameron chimes in, then Tegan adds, "She takes for-freaking-ever."

"Anyway." Kim clears her throat. "When I stepped out of the bathroom I found a note on the bed. One Morgan *actually* wrote this time."

The joke makes us all chuckle, except for Morgan who rolls his eyes. "Continue, smart *ash*."

Kim kisses him on the cheek, twisting the ring. "It said 'You're already the most beautiful woman on this planet, but humor me. Put this on and meet me by the Christmas Tree.'" She looks down, a shyness to her that I'm not used to. But I would bet any amount of money Morgan has this look of hers memorized. "Under the note was a gorgeous black gown. Obviously I put it on, not before fixing my hair up a bit of course, I'm not an idiot. I knew he was up to something."

"What can I say? I'm a devious creature," Morgan kids.

"So what happened next?" Elodie surprises us by asking, even if she is looking down at her hands.

"Kim looked like a beautiful princess when she appeared in the living room," Daniel answers for us, smiling slightly at Kim. "She was very happy."

"I was, Danny," Kim confirms. "I'm still so happy to become a part of your family."

"You already are," he responds. "You're the sister I never had."

This brings tears to Kim's eyes, Cameron and Tegan's too.

Me? I swear I'm smelling onions from the kitchen.

"Love you baby bro." Kim winks at him.

"Continue, filha, before your friends here start asking to use my cut as a Kleenex."

That comment is enough to break the emotional tension, and allow Kim to get back to her story.

"When I walked out of the bedroom I found the entire house adorned in candles, a trail of black roses leading me to the Christmas tree, where Morgan was standing next to a lit up sign saying "Will you *merry* me, Kimberly Pereira?""

"You know, for Merry Christ—" Morgan tries to explain.

"Yeah we got that brainiac." Tegan blows her nose with a tissue, courtesy of Loretta. "Let her finish, we need to hear the rest!"

Morgan holds up two hands in defense, allowing his fiancée to continue.

"When I approached Morgan I was shaking, he was too if I'm being honest."

Morgan blows out a deep breath, half joking as he says, "It was a lot of work to put in for a girl to say no, ya know?"

"I would never, stupid." Kim pushes him, continuing once again, "But when I saw the ring next to Stella's portrait above the fireplace, I lost it. Then, when Morgan started his speech, my father and Loretta appearing, it all became one big beautiful blur. Before I knew it my arms were wrapped around him and we were kissing, the photographer snapping pictures, and our brothers popping confetti over us."

"It was absolutely magical," Loretta announces. "Everything was perfect."

"It really was." Kim scoots closer to Morgan, even though she's practically on his lap. "I couldn't have imagined a better way to say hell yeah."

"Here's to hell yeah!" I shout, picking up a glass of champagne, nodding for everyone else to do the same. "To the soon-to-be Mr. and Mrs. Brookes. I can't imagine a crazier couple crazier for each other than these two. Congratulations, guys."

We all raise our glasses and cheer to their happiness.

Wishing them a lifetime and more of it.

DINNER PASSES WITH A MIX OF GOOD FOOD, LAUGHS, terrible jokes, and awesome jabs aimed for no other than the man of the hour Morgan.

The kids' tiredness is slowly creeping in from the long day so as Cameron, Tegan, and Kim get the kiddos ready for bed, the rest of us, minus Sayeed and Sam who cut out after dinner, sit around the living room shooting the shit before doing our annual Secret Santa gift exchange.

We talk mostly about new projects at work, updates in life, and even Marcos joins in with some upcoming renovations at his bar.

I'm just finishing up explaining a new house renovation I've been working on when the girls reappear in the living room like they just trekked hours through No Man's Land.

"Kids asleep?" I ask Cameron as she collapses next to me on the couch.

"After that fight, they better be." She groans, resting her head back on the couch.

Cameron looks…exhausted. I know she's worked her ass off today but by the way I'm watching her energy deplete before me tells me it may be something else.

I hope she's feeling alright.

I reach over and brush some hair from her forehead. "You good, Nyx?"

"I'm fine, babe. Just the repercussions of a busy day."

Accepting her answer, I reach down on the floor and pick up each of our gifts for the exchange.

Marcos and Loretta wander into the kitchen together to leave us to it as usual. Loretta insists on cleaning up after us, still unable to let go of the housekeeper title she's grown so used to throughout the years. I'm grateful for it now since I can see how tired Cameron is.

"So, let me start by saying my reason for forgetting to get my gift this year is totally valid."

An eruption of complaints follows his defense, and a "you really are the worst" comes from Tegan.

"I was a bit preoccupied picking out a ring. It slipped my mind, alright?"

"Well, lucky for you I've anticipated this very situation, and took it upon myself to grab a gift for your Secret Santa." Cameron reaches under the coffee table and pulls out a small gift bag.

"How the hell do you know who my Secret Santa is?" Morgan quirks an eyebrow.

All three girls shoot him a look like *are you serious?*

They do the math amongst themselves every year, hoping none of their names are on Morgan's paper.

"I appreciate that, Cam." Morgan reaches for the gift but she tsks-tsks him with a wave of her finger.

"Nuh-uh. I never said the gift was meant to be from you. You sit on your throne of shame over there. I'll be giving it to my husband. Thank you very much."

Morgan waves her off and watches as each of us hand gifts to their fellow recipients.

A large box for Tegan from Kim. A pretty golden bag for Cameron from Tegan. A poorly wrapped red present for Austin from Cameron, and so on until everyone, except me of course because my Secret Santa sucks, is holding a gift in front of them.

"I'll give you yours at the end, okay?" Cameron reassures me and I nod, not really giving a shit about gifts anyway. I just thoroughly enjoy busting Morgan's balls.

"Alright bitches! Open!" Tegan announces, then rips open her present.

Everybody else follows suit.

"Oh my God! This is the makeup case I've been wanting!" Tegan hugs the box to her chest. "Kimmy I love it so much! Thank you."

Kim winks at her. "I gotchu my little capuchin, you know that." Opening up her thin wrapped present, Kim's eyes light up when she sees what Austin got her. "Holy shit! Yes!" She presents the gift to us, revealing a Metallica Vinyl. "Thanks Texas, I guess I'll keep you."

"As if you got a choice, lady. You love me."

"It's unfortunate, but true." She reaches for him, playfully punching his knee.

After everyone shows off what they got, Tegan the makeup kit, Kim the vinyl, Austin a pair of cowboy boots, Cameron a new bag, and Morgan a wallet, Cameron finally hands me the small bag she set aside as a "just in case" Morgan pulls, well, *a Morgan*.

"I felt it appropriate to save the best present for last." Cameron sticks her tongue out at Morgan, where he returns the sentiment doing the same.

"Whatcha got for me here, Nyx?" I shake the bag, teasing her. "It's pretty small, you tryin' to tell me something?"

"Sounds like you should open it and find out."

The room goes silent as I stuff my hand in the bag, pulling out a long box, similar to one that would hold a bracelet.

"Jewelry?" I question, since it's not unlike her to randomly get me an outrageously expensive piece of gold or silver.

"I doubt you'd want to wear this around. Just open it."

"Yeah, man. Just open it," Morgan insists. "I'm curious to know what I got you."

With an eye roll his way, I lift the box open just enough to see exactly what's inside, then instinctively slam it shut. "No fucking way."

Cameron smiles, nodding her head.

This explains everything:

The refusal of wine.

Exhaustion.

Glowing skin.

"Fuck yes!" I jump up out of my seat and scoop Cameron in my arms, spinning her around as I kiss every inch of her face.

"Are you happy?" she whispers in my ear.

"I'm absolutely ecstatic, baby."

"Uhm, hello! We'd like to join in on the cheer," Kim complains. "What the hell is in that box?"

"Yeah, and shouldn't you be hugging yours truly? Since technically the gift was from me?" Morgan argues with his arms wide.

Placing Cameron down on the floor, I open up the box one final time and pull out the white stick, holding it out for everyone to see.

"I'm gonna be a dad again, guys."

Cheers fill the room as everyone except Daniel and his date stands, forming a huddle around my wife and me.

"We're having another baby!" Tegan squeaks, squeezing her arm around my back as Morgan deadpans, "Can somebody say breeding kink?"

Such. A. Dick.

"Will you name this one Darrell if it's a boy?" Kim asks, actually hopeful. "I mean…I doubt Dime is an option."

Cameron and I share widened eyes before she says, "Uh, maybe?"

Uh, how about *never*.

"You guys are literally going to have an empire of kids soon." Morgan laughs. "They can make a TV show about you. Call it 'The Cartashians' or some shit."

We all stare unamused at Morgan, who is smiling with a gleam as if he's waiting for everyone to agree with him.

We don't, obviously.

I wonder how a man who isn't a dad comes up with the most asinine dad jokes?

"Let's get me past the first trimester before we go planning names and television series," Cameron says, adding, "Our life is hectic enough."

I swoop an arm behind Cameron, bringing her into me again. "You are a literal fucking goddess, Nyx. You've given me everything I ever wanted."

"I can say the same for you, mister." She bumps her nose with mine. "After all, it takes two to make one of these." She presses a hand to her belly.

I place my palm over hers. "But it's because of you that they're as awesome as they are."

"So what do you think of Daniel, Elodie?" Tegan chirps, taking a sip of her cappuccino.

The night is coming to an end, and by now most of the table is cleaned up and the kitchen is spotless thanks to the wonderful Loretta.

It takes about a half hour of baby talk, predicting due dates, genders, and eye color before the subject finally makes a change.

I'm still trying to absorb the fact we have baby number four on the way.

A big family is what I always wanted, and thanks to my beautiful wife, and a couple neat new sex positions, a big family is what I'll be getting.

It's been a ton of great news for everyone tonight, including announcing Cameron's adoption of Emersyn.

We've given more than enough time for our new guest to get comfortable before we started drilling her with some easy questions.

"Daniel has been very nice to me, he loves talking to me about the ocean," Elodie says rather sheepishly.

"I hope he's making time to talk about some of the things you like, too," Morgan responds.

Elodie shrugs, looking down at her cup of sparkling grape juice. "I like whatever Daniel likes."

The "awwww's" are imminent after this statement. Mostly from Cameron and Tegan as they continue to adore Daniel's date.

"Elodie enjoys music like you, Kim," Daniel admits. "She likes using the Beats you gave me to listen to Coldplay."

Kim looks as though she's ten centimeters dilated as she smiles at Elodie. "That's...great. Coldplay is just...great."

I've seen better lies come from crooked politicians.

Morgan hits her thigh, and she adds, "Sounds like Daniel knows what to get you next Christmas."

"Just his friendship is enough for me," Elodie counters.

That does it, Tegan and Cameron are officially melted puddles on the floor.

"Well you're welcome over at the house anytime dear," Loretta cuts in. "Any time."

"Okay. I will be there tomorrow then," Elodie replies plainly. "Around three o'clock for *Shark Tank*."

Well, damn, she's as literal as Daniel, only cuter and less demanding.

At least for now.

Daniel shifts on his seat, the smallest glint of excitement in his eyes.

I'm happy for him.

For all of us.

Each and every person in this room has been through hell, but made it out the gates even better than before.

There's nothing like the holidays to remind you where you came from, and how far you've come.

It's a real sense of catharsis to watch the people you love growing and succeeding. Overcoming the obstacles they once thought would be in their way forever.

Life is funny that way, one moment you're at your lowest, and the next you have five pairs of hands lifting you up.

Calling you family.

Making the world right again.

It's something I will never take for granted, no matter what this life has in store for us.

"So, what's next in our story guys?" Tegan asks, wrapping her arms around Kim and Cameron. "Any guesses?"

I shrug, looking around the living room at the only family I've ever had, and the only girl left to find herself a soul mate.

I've never hated and loved an idea as much as I do this.

Tegan has not only become the group's most cherished tiny human, but she's also become the backbone in which our crew stands.

Without her, there really is no us.

And without her happiness, there really is no her. So it's only a matter of time before I have to accept there's some asshole out there good enough for her.

But until then, I will be making sure no motherfucker dares to break her heart.

That's all tomorrow's problems, though, because all I want to do tonight is get my hands on Cameron's cranberry pie.

Then turn up the Christmas tunes, and break the news about the carols that these assholes will be forced to sing with Emersyn's karaoke microphone.

I didn't lie when I said I wanted to be as obnoxious as possible on my favorite holiday.

I mean, it's only fair since Morgan is obnoxious the other 364 days out of the year.

This is my time to shine, baby. And there is no real merry in a Christmas unless it's a Carter Christmas.

Ugly sweater and all.

AFTERWORD

Hey everybody! I hope you enjoyed reading this little holiday story, I know I missed my man Jaxon so much. I loved getting back in his head.

Wishing all my readers a Merry Christmas, Happy Holidays, and a wonderful New Year.

Stay tuned for what's to come in 2023!

ABOUT THE AUTHOR

Danda K.

is a new Romance Author originally from New York City but now residing in the Garden State.

She's also a wife and mother to three wild little boys. She got her name Danda from her niece and nephew's who are practically her own kids. She's awkward, as thirsty as they come, and her obsession with her cats will never go unnoticed. You'll likely find her hiding snacks from her kids, binge watching Netflix, or reading. Books give her life, and now she focuses her short attention span on writing her own stories. She may still reside in a busy city but spends most of her time at home avoiding people and hanging out with fictional characters. She has dipped her pen in poetry since she was a little girl but found a love for writing romance. Thankful for her early readers, she enjoys engaging with them and sharing her love for books and favorite authors.

You can email Danda K. with any questions or comments at :
Dandakauthor@gmail.com

Follow my Facebook page for news on what's next:
https://smarturl.it/DKfbp

Join my Facebook group : https://smarturl.it/DKbookbabes

Check out my website : www.Dandakauthor.com

ALSO BY DANDA K

The Ties Duet:

The Ties That Bind Us (Part 1)

The Ties That Bind Us (Part 2)

Savage Love Duet:

You Broke Me First

You Loved Me First